Clipper's Crazy Race

Doug and Debbie Kingsriter

Illustrated by Ann Iosa

WORD kids!

WORD PUBLISHING
Dallas·London·Vancouver·Melbourne

Our thanks to:
Laura Minchew for believing that
all of us need to care for God's Earth;
Laura Minchew and Brenda Ward for creating this
book series to encourage little and big people alike
to do what we can to be good stewards of our world;
and all the children who are teaching us, by example,
to take care of God's beautiful earth.

Other Books in the
Save God's Earth Series:

Gilroy's Goof
Finny's Big Break

Clipper's Crazy Race
Copyright © 1992 by Doug and Debbie Kingsriter for the text.
Copyright © 1992 by Ann Iosa for the illustrations.

Library of Congress Cataloging-in-Publication Data

Kingsriter, Debbie, 1951–
  Clipper's Crazy Race / by Debbie and Doug Kingsriter; illustrated
by Ann Iosa.
    p. cm. — (Save God's Earth)
  Summary: Clipper the Cloud turns green from the smog in her formerly blue skies, and it takes the hard work of the town animals and people to help her regain her health.
  ISBN 0–8499–0921–X
  [1. Clouds—Fiction. 2. Animals—Fiction. 3. Air—Pollution—Fiction 4. Pollution—Fiction.] I. Kingsriter, Doug. II. Iosa, Ann, ill. III. Title. IV. Series: Kingsriter, Debbie. 1951– Save God's Earth
  PZ7.K618Cl 1992
  [E]—dc20   92–12327
                                                                                 CIP
                                                                                  AC

Printed in the United States of America

2345679 LBM 987654321

To our children,
Lauren, Barrett, and Blake,
but especially Lauren who is a shining star
and whose smile has brightened
our lives like the sun

More than anything else, Clipper the Cloud loved to play in the blue skies over Hilldale. Clipper looked quite ordinary. She was fluffy and had big dimples when she smiled. But there was something special about Clipper you couldn't see . . . her imagination!

Sometimes the sky was Clipper's stage and she was a graceful ballerina. At other times she was a champion ice skater speeding ahead of the other clouds. When the sky looked like the ocean, Clipper was a dangerous shark with fierce teeth. Well, as fierce as a cloud can get.

Clipper liked to make the children of Hilldale happy by changing shapes. On school days she'd sail above Celebration Hill.

"Oh, look!" the kids would holler when Clipper made herself look like a big puppy sitting up to beg. Then they'd laugh when Clipper turned into a hopping kangaroo. That always made the kids want to hop, too.

But racing was what Clipper liked best. Every day she'd race Hawk, Crow, and Bluejay. Clipper loved the feeling of fresh air against her face.

One day Hawk suggested they race to Milltown and back. Milltown was a place with many factories, not far from Hilldale. It was just the right distance for a good race.

"First one back to the tree wins," screeched Bluejay.

"On your mark," squawked Hawk.

"Get set," cawed Crow.

"GO!" yelled Clipper, and off they flew.

Clipper took the lead, flying high above the highway. Factory smoke lay like a blanket over Milltown. The air smelled awful. Clipper's eyes and nose burned. It was getting hard to breathe.

As the racers headed back to Hilldale, Clipper started to cough. She began to lose speed.

Maybe I'm sailing too high, Clipper thought. She floated closer to the highway. But the exhaust from the cars made her cough more. Finally, she just had to stop. She couldn't continue the race.

Hawk, Bluejay, and Crow flew back to see what had happened.

"You don't look so good," said Crow. "You look green."

Indeed, Clipper did look green . . . and yellow . . . and brown. Something was wrong.

"I don't feel so good," coughed Clipper.

Hawk put his wing on Clipper. "Let's finish the race another day," he said.

Bluejay, Crow, and Hawk carried Clipper back to Hilldale. She coughed the whole way.

"Maybe if you go real high, the wind will blow that stuff off," said Bluejay.

"I can't get any higher," puffed Clipper. "I feel too heavy."

Clipper was frightened because she'd heard about clouds getting smog. Clouds that got smog couldn't fly. They couldn't race or make fun shapes either. Clouds with smog looked bad.

"I'm going to get Dr. Pelican," offered Hawk. "Maybe she can help." Dr. Pelican was the doctor for all the birds.

Clipper started to cry.

"There, there," comforted Crow. "Why don't you make a happy shape? It'll make you feel better."

Clipper tried to make an airplane, but all she could do was cough.

When Dr. Pelican saw Clipper, she sadly shook her head. "You are a very sick cloud."

"I've never been sick before," said Clipper.

"Clouds aren't supposed to get sick," replied Dr. Pelican. "Say ah-h-h-h."

Clipper's throat looked very green. Dr. Pelican listened to Clipper's breathing with her cloudoscope. What she heard sounded like a woodpecker tapping on a tree.

"Well, Clipper," said the doctor, as she took off her glasses. "You've breathed too much bad air. I'm afraid you've got smog."

Clipper was very sad.

"This is terrible," moaned Bluejay.

Dr. Pelican continued. "The only way you can get well is to breathe lots of good air, Clipper. And please, no more trips over the factories."

When Dr. Pelican left, Hawk, Crow, and Bluejay gathered around Clipper. "We're going to help you get well!" said Crow. "It's no use. I'm never going to fly again," said Clipper sadly. "Yes you will," screeched Bluejay. "We'll think of something."

"Let's take Clipper to Celebration Hill," suggested Hawk. "Maybe there's something the kids can do."

Clipper's three friends pushed and pulled with all their might. Finally they got Clipper up the hill. She was so heavy, it was all she could do to stay on top of the hill. How Clipper wished she could fly again!

On the playground below, Laura, Ben, and their grandfather watched the curious sight.

"That cloud looks awful," exclaimed Laura.

"It sure does," said Grandfather. "Let's get a closer look."

When the children and Grandfather reached the top of the hill, their lungs and eyes were burning.

"This cloud is bad news," said Ben. "How do you think it got this way, Grandfather?"

"I think this is a man-made problem, Ben," replied Grandfather. "Lots of good things are made in factories. But factory smoke and car exhaust get trapped in clouds. That's what happened to this cloud."

"Is there a way to get the smoke out?" asked Laura.

"I think I can answer your question at the fruit orchard," said Grandfather with a smile. Grandfather had beautiful gardens and fruit trees on his farm. It was a fun place to go. Ben and Laura quickly followed Grandfather down the hill.

"I love plants and trees," said Grandfather. "That's what God made on the third day of creation. And He caused each one of them to make seeds so we can keep on enjoying what He created."

"Like apples," said Laura.

"That's right. But plants and trees also help us in ways we can't see," replied Grandfather. "God made each tree and plant with a special ability to turn bad air into good air."

"Why is that cloud on Celebration Hill so dirty?" asked Ben.

"We have put more smoke and auto exhaust into the air than plants can take out," Grandfather said, shaking his head.

"So what we need is more trees and plants," said Laura.

"And less smoke and exhaust," added Grandfather.

"Say, I've got an idea!" said Laura, suddenly excited. "We can plant some trees on Celebration Hill to save that cloud!"

"Do you think it'll work, Grandfather?" asked Ben.

"It's worth a try," said Grandfather. "I have plenty of small trees you can have."

Laura and Ben invited other kids to their planting party. They placed signs around town that read, "Clean Air Fair at Celebration Hill." Soon the hill was covered with kids, wheelbarrows, shovels, and . . . TREES!

Clipper liked having the kids walk through her. It kind of tickled. She remembered how she used to make them laugh. And she wanted to do it again. She wanted to be clean and healthy. She did not want to have smog.

Hawk, Bluejay, and Crow watched the big tree-planting event from a nearby oak. As soon as the kids left, Clipper's three friends hurried to her.

"Breathe the good air. That's what the Doctor said," squawked Hawk.

"I told you we could help," bragged Bluejay.

Clipper inhaled the good air from the trees and rested.
It takes a long time to cure smog. But every day, Clipper got a little better. The trees were absorbing the smoke and exhaust that had made her so sick.

One morning when Clipper was still asleep, Bluejay cried out, "Look! Clipper's changing color!"
Sure enough, Clipper wasn't so green anymore.

Just then Clipper awakened to the screechy-scratchy sounds of Hawk, Crow, and Bluejay. They were circling around her. "Wake up, you big cotton ball," called Crow.

"Time to make some funny cloud shapes!" announced Bluejay.

Clipper looked down at the town of Hilldale far below. "I'm flying!" she cheered . . . and so was her imagination. Clipper hopped, skipped, and jumped—all at the same time! She made every animal shape she could think of. She even did a cartwheel!

On their way to school, the children rushed up Celebration Hill to get a better view. And a very happy Clipper said "thank you" with the greatest cloud show ever performed.

Things You Can Do

- Plant a garden, plant a tree, or both. Oxygen released from growing plants and trees helps clean the air.

- Try using a living Christmas tree this year instead of cutting one down, and then plant it in your yard.

- Ask your parents not to buy products in aerosol spray cans. The gas in these cans is harmful to the ozone layer in our atmosphere.

- Ride your bike or walk instead of riding in the car. If you do need to ride in the car, then carpool. You'll be reducing the amount of auto exhaust that pollutes the air.

- Ask your parents to turn down your thermostat in the winter to 65° F, and keep your summer air conditioning at 78° F. If every home in the United States reduced their heat in the winter by six degrees, we would save 500,000 barrels of oil each day!